Jan Pieńkowski

Bel and Bub

and the Black Hole

A Dorling Kindersley Book

It was a lovely day.
The stars were shining.

Bel and Bub wanted to play.

Bel and Bub ran out of
the house.

They raced down the path . . .

Shall we let Draco out?

. . . to the black hole where Draco lived.

They could hear snoring.

As Bub opened the lock
Draco woke up.

Dinner-time,
he thought.

The door flew open
and hit Bub on the head.

Draco burst out.

Bel ran away.

Where's Bel?

Bub couldn't see Bel anywhere.
Draco was enjoying himself.

He was gobbling up all the stars in the Milky Way.

Draco's tummy was HUGE.
Had he eaten Bel as well?

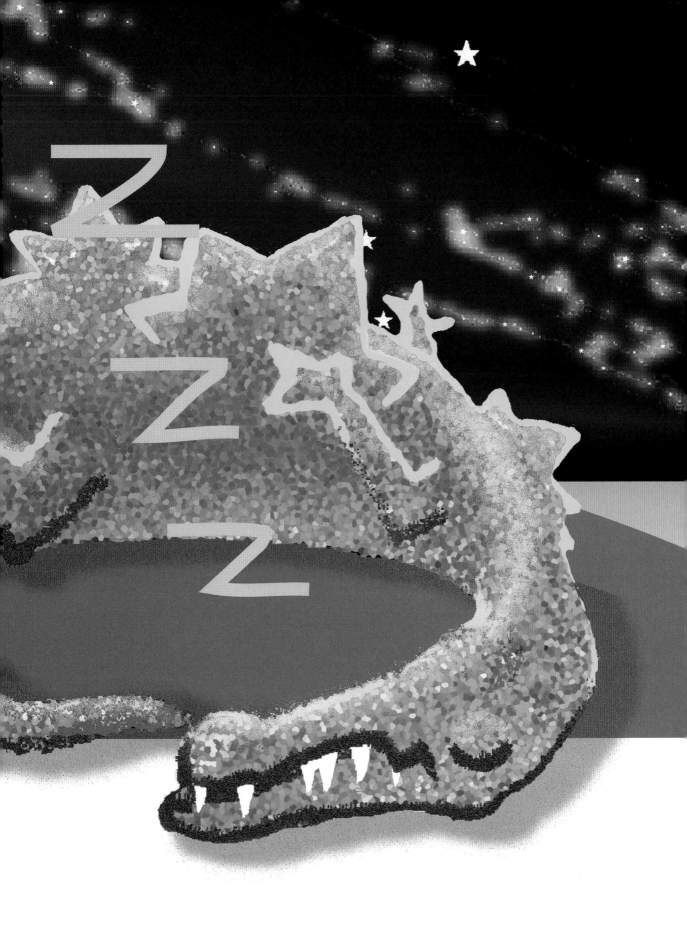

Bub jumped on Draco's tummy. Stars popped out . . .

. . . burp, burp! But no Bel.

Bub went home. He brought back Bel's feather.

It was a sad day.

Suddenly they heard a roar.
Bel burst through the door.

She was dragging Draco in!

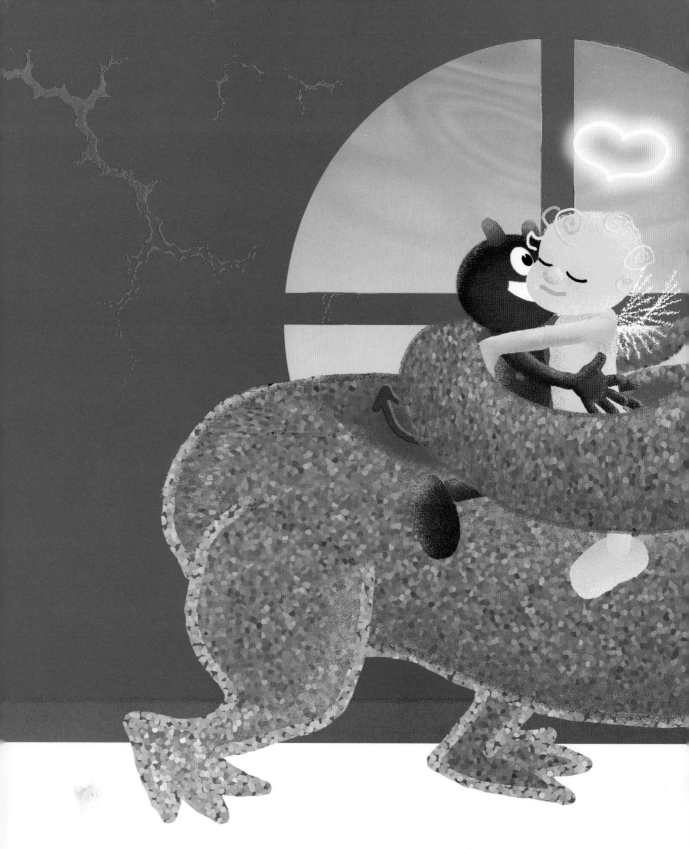

There were hugs and kisses.

Draco got a cookie.

They went back to the black hole.

See you tomorrow!

Draco was happy to be home.

That night they had their favorite story read to them.